SY 0033312 3

D0246759

ST. MARY'S COLLEGE
LIBRARY

FALLS ROAD

40383

3

X

# THE USBORNE FIRST BOOK OF FRANCE

## Louisa Somerville
### with
### Béatrice Rios and Camille Pataut

### Illustrated by Roger Fereday
### Designed by Mary Cartwright
### Edited by Cheryl Evans

## Contents

With thanks to Annick Dunbar and to
Christine Fenley and the French Government Tourist Office.

# Map of France

France is the largest country in Western Europe. It is surrounded by both land and sea. This map shows you how varied the scenery is in different parts of the country.

## Words in French

You will find some French words in this book printed in italics like this, *moules.* Each word is explained, or the English for it is shown in brackets, for example *moules* (mussels).

### Facts about France

The population of France is about 55 million.

The capital city is Paris.

The five largest cities are in order, Paris, Lyon, Marseille, Lille and Bordeaux.

The highest mountain is Mont Blanc. At 4,807m it is also the highest mountain in Europe.

The longest river is the River Loire. It flows for 1,020km.

## France and Europe

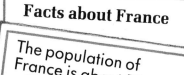

France is in the continent of Europe. It is a member of the European Community (EC). The countries of the EC are coloured green on the map above.

Ferries cross the Channel to England from these ports.

Cherbourg

ENGLISH CHANNEL

ATLANTIC OCEAN

On the Atlantic coast there are lots of fishing ports and long, sandy beaches with huge, rolling waves.

Bordeaux

## The shape of France

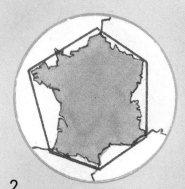

France has six sides. It has three land borders and three coasts. Mountains form a border on two sides and the sea on three more.
   The sixth side, the north-east, has no natural border. This made it easy in the past for people to invade.

The airports most used by holidaymakers are shown on the map like this.

2

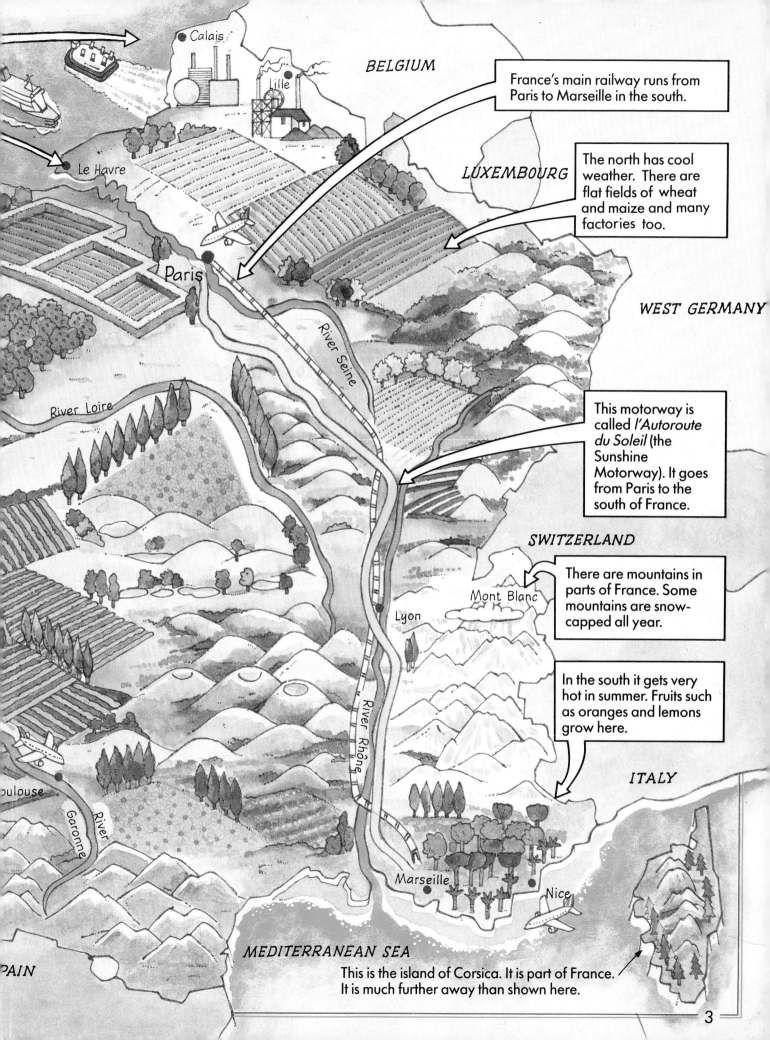

Calais

BELGIUM

France's main railway runs from Paris to Marseille in the south.

Le Havre

Lille

LUXEMBOURG

The north has cool weather. There are flat fields of wheat and maize and many factories too.

WEST GERMANY

Paris

River Seine

River Loire

This motorway is called *l'Autoroute du Soleil* (the Sunshine Motorway). It goes from Paris to the south of France.

SWITZERLAND

Mont Blanc

There are mountains in parts of France. Some mountains are snow-capped all year.

Lyon

In the south it gets very hot in summer. Fruits such as oranges and lemons grow here.

ITALY

oulouse

Garonne River

River Rhône

Marseille

Nice

PAIN

MEDITERRANEAN SEA

This is the island of Corsica. It is part of France. It is much further away than shown here.

3

# Life at home and school

The French have their own ways of doing everyday things. You may find some customs on these two pages are the same as yours, while others may be quite different.

## Sébastien's day

My name is Sébastien and I am ten years old. I get up at half past seven, when Dad leaves for work. I wear what I like as there is no school uniform.

It's a rush in the morning so for breakfast I just have a *tartine* (slice of bread and butter). I like dipping it in a bowl of hot chocolate.

## Saying hello

When French people meet, they always shake hands, or kiss if they are friends or relatives. The number of kisses depends on the area they come from.

People in the south kiss once on each cheek. People from Paris give three kisses. In the north they kiss four times, twice on each cheek.

School starts at half past eight. We leave my little sister Marie at the nursery school first. I went there too, until I was six.

These are my friends Romain, Abdul and Pedro. Abdul was born in Algeria and Pedro comes from Spain, but they both live in France now.

## Wednesdays

For most children there is no school on Wednesdays. This used to be a day for religious studies.

Nowadays many children play sport or go to clubs, such as scouts.

Those who live near the mountains may go skiing on Wednesdays.

## The week-end

Children go to school on Saturday morning. They probably spend the rest of the week-end with friends and family.

Many families visit relatives on Sundays. Sunday lunch is a special meal that may last for hours.

## Eating French style

Here are some tips on eating like French people.

Tuck your napkin in at the neck. This helps when you eat sloppy food like soup or spaghetti.

Keep your hands on the table, not in your lap.

Hold your fork in your right hand. Push food onto it with bread held in your left hand.

Use bread to mop up any delicious sauce.

Keep the same knife and fork till the end of your meal.

### Bread and wine

At lunch and supper there is always plenty of bread on the table and everyone helps themselves.
Many people drink wine or mineral water with their meal.

We have two playtimes each day. Some children play hopscotch and skip with elastic, but we prefer football or marbles.

We have a long lunch break of two hours. I go home, but Romain and Abdullah eat in the school canteen because their mothers are at work.

We go home at half past four. Look at my bulging satchel. The teacher always gives us lots of homework.

When I get home, I like to eat a chunk of bread with a piece of chocolate while I watch my favourite television programme.

## Sébastien's house

Like many French houses, Sébastien's house has a garage and a utility room downstairs. All the living rooms are upstairs.

The windows open inwards so they can be kept open when the shutters are closed.

Shutters keep the house warm in winter and cool in summer.

An outside staircase leads to the front door.

On fine days the bedding is aired on the balcony.

We have supper at seven o'clock, when Dad gets home. When I go to bed, I read my cartoon book, The Adventures of Asterix the Gaul.

# Food and drink

France is famous for its delicious food and wines. The French are proud of their food and spend a lot of time preparing it. Both boys and girls learn to cook when they are young.

The leaves of a boiled artichoke can be dipped in melted butter or oil and vinegar dressing. Only the bottom of each leaf is eaten.

NORMANDY

Snails are cooked with garlic butter.

CHAMPAGNE

BRITTANY

Champagne is a fizzy white wine, drunk on special occasions.

BURGUNDY

Grapes grow in vineyards all over France. Bordeaux is one famous wine-growing area.

Fondue savoyarde is eaten in the Alps. It is hot melted cheese and white wine, into which you dip cubes of bread.

SAVOIE

On the coast of Brittany, mussels are picked off the rocks. They are sometimes cooked in white wine.

BORDEAUX

More than 350 kinds of cheese are made in France. A famous one is Roquefort. It is left in underground caves until it is ready to eat.

Roquefort

Olives grow in Provence. Many are crushed to make olive oil.

PROVENCE

## How wine is made

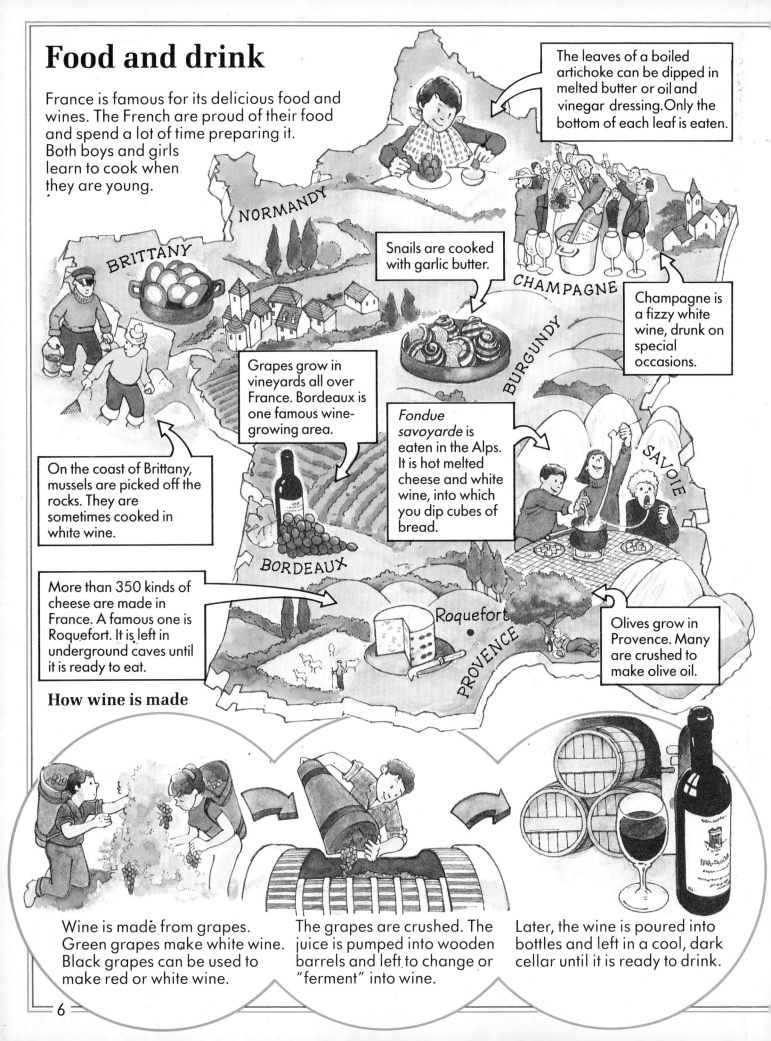

Wine is made from grapes. Green grapes make white wine. Black grapes can be used to make red or white wine.

The grapes are crushed. The juice is pumped into wooden barrels and left to change or "ferment" into wine.

Later, the wine is poured into bottles and left in a cool, dark cellar until it is ready to drink.

## The café

French people often go to cafés to have a snack or just a drink. There are usually tables outside for you to sit at when it is warm.

This mint syrup and lemonade drink is called *diabolo-menthe* (devil's mint).

Strong black coffee is served in tiny cups. Sugar cubes are put on the saucer.

A French sandwich can be tricky to eat. It is usually half a *baguette* (a long, crusty loaf) filled with cheese or ham.

## A French drink to make

On hot days, people sip a refreshing lemon drink called *citron pressé*.

To make it, squeeze the juice of a lemon into a glass. Fill to the top with cold water and ice cubes. Stir in some sugar to sweeten it.

## Food fables

King Henry IV was known as Henry the Good. He made France wealthy, so even poor people could afford chicken in the pot every Sunday.

Tarte Tatin is named after a restaurant owner called Madame Tatin. She dropped an apple tart upside down on her stove.

The top burnt to caramel and the tart tasted even better.

## How to make Tarte Tatin

100g soft butter
100g brown sugar
3 apples
150g packet of shortcrust or puff pastry
Set the oven to 220c / 425F / Gas mark 7

◀ Spread the butter over the bottom of a 20cm flan tin.

◀ Sprinkle over the sugar.

◀ Peel, core and slice the apples. Arrange them in the tin.

◀ Roll out the pastry. Lay it over the apples and press the edges in so it fits inside the tin.

◀ Bake the tart in the oven for about 40 minutes, until it is golden brown.

◀ Put a plate on top of the tin and turn it over, so the caramel runs over the tart. Wear oven gloves as the tin will be hot.

You can eat Tarte Tatin hot or cold, with cream if you like.

7

# French towns and countryside

Many towns have a main square where you will find shops, cafés and tourist information. This is usually the oldest part of the town.

Modern houses and blocks of flats are built on the outskirts of the town.

Some people live in flats in very old buildings with balconies and shutters, built round a courtyard.

The French flag flies outside the town hall.

The *concierge* (caretaker) looks after all the flats in a block. He or she knows each tenant and all the gossip.

People can win big prizes in the national lottery. They buy tickets from kiosks and bars.

Post boxes are yellow.

A stone monument is in memory of those who died in the two world wars.

Many old streets are cobbled. You get a bumpy ride in a car.

The chemist's shop has a green cross outside.

In wide streets, cars may be parked facing the pavement.

Cafés stay open from early morning to late at night. People drop in to meet friends.

A red cigar-shaped sign is above the tobacconist's. Stamps are sold here too.

## Some unusual towns

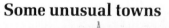

An abbey was built on the island of Mont-St-Michel nearly 1,000 years ago. A town grew up around it. You can get to the island by a raised road.

Carcassonne has been rebuilt to look like it did in the Middle Ages. It has ramparts, drawbridges, a moat and a castle.

Le Puy is a town built round peaks of hard, volcanic rock. Hundreds of steps carved in the rock lead to the chapel at the top.

## Roofs

You can sometimes tell which part of France a building is in, by looking at its roof.

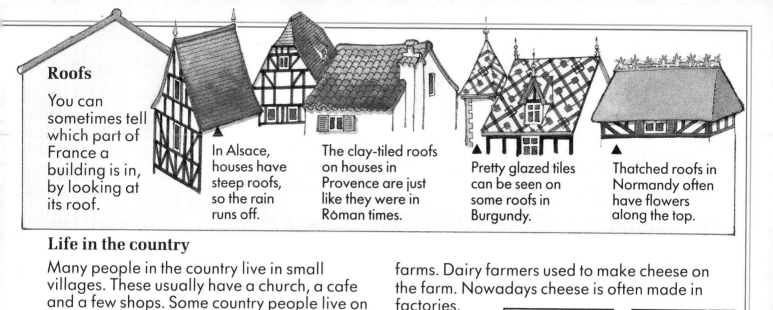

In Alsace, houses have steep roofs, so the rain runs off.

The clay-tiled roofs on houses in Provence are just like they were in Roman times.

Pretty glazed tiles can be seen on some roofs in Burgundy.

Thatched roofs in Normandy often have flowers along the top.

## Life in the country

Many people in the country live in small villages. These usually have a church, a cafe and a few shops. Some country people live on farms. Dairy farmers used to make cheese on the farm. Nowadays cheese is often made in factories.

## Cheese-making

In the mountains, farmers make cheese from goat and sheep's milk in summer. They sell it at markets in the autumn.

Sour milk and rennet (an acid) are added to milk so it thickens. Next it is cut and put in moulds.

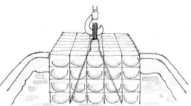

Slowly, the whey (liquid) drains away from the curds (solids). Sometimes salt is now added.

The curds are left to dry out. Soon a rind grows on the outside. The cheese ripens inside.

## Animals

You may see these animals in country areas. Some are extremely rare.

Wild boar are sometimes hunted in the forests.

Storks nest on rooftops and chimneys all over Alsace.

Trained pigs or dogs search for truffles. These are a rare sort of fungi, which people eat.

Wild goats, called chamois, live in the Alps. They are very shy.

In the mountains, cattle wear bells so farmers can hear them far away.

You might be lucky and see a golden eagle soaring over the mountains.

Flocks of pink flamingoes live in the marshes of the Camargue.

On summer nights in Provence, you can hear a high-pitched hissing noise. This is made by insects called cicadas.

# Travelling in France

There are many different ways of getting about in France. However, in country areas there are few buses, so most French people own a car. If you are travelling in France, see how many of the things on these two pages you can spot.

You must pay to use most motorways. Look for the *péage* (toll) sign.

Lorries and coaches have speed limits shown by a sticker on the back.

These arrows are for holiday routes. They are pleasant, quiet roads.

Sometimes a policeman directs traffic from the middle of the road.

Traffic lights go straight from red to green. Amber shows when the lights are returning to red.

Anyone over the age of 14 can ride a moped. Lots of pupils ride them to school.

Most French people like to drive French cars. Renault, Peugeot and Citroën are popular makes.

People drive on the right-hand side of the road.

### Historic French firsts

◀ The Montgolfier brothers invented the hot-air balloon in 1783. The first passengers were a duck, a sheep and a cockerel.

Louis Blériot was ▶ the first person to fly across water. He crossed the English Channel in 1909.

The Citroën 2CV is one of the best-known cars. It is often called the *Deux Chevaux* (two horses) because it has a two "horse-power" engine. It is no longer made in France.

## Record breakers

The supersonic airliner Concorde, was built jointly by French and British companies. It is the fastest passenger plane in the world. It flies between Paris and New York in under four hours.

The TGV, short for *Train à Grande Vitesse* (High Speed Train), is the fastest train in the world. Its record speed is 380km per hour.

It only runs on main routes as it needs special tracks.

Before you go on to the platform, you must punch your ticket in a machine.

The French are proud of their trains. They are fast and nearly always on time.

Station platforms are low, so trains have steps up to them.

This sign shows the times of local church services.

Towns and villages have a name sign. As you leave, there is another name sign with a line through it.

## Travel in Paris

The Paris underground railway is called the Métro, (short for Métropolitain). The stations are named after famous places and people such as Victor Hugo, a writer.

Some stations have old decorated entrance signs.

A sign shows where to wait to get into a first class carriage.

There is one first class carriage.

The trains are quiet because they run on rubber tyres.

You use the same tickets on buses and Métro trains.

18894 C RATP 2 METRO AUTOBUS 766A62

## Buses

The buses in Paris are green and white.

A map at the bus stop tells you where you are on the route and the names of the stops.

Some buses in busy areas have two joined compartments.

Usually you buy a ticket before you board the bus. Punch your ticket in the machine as you enter.

Some goods are still transported by canal because it is cheap. The bargeman lives on the barge.

During the grape harvest you may pass trucks laden with grapes. It is the custom to wave to the grape pickers.

# Holidays

Most French people go on holiday in August. The roads, beaches and campsites get very crowded. Some children go to *colonies de vacances,* children's holiday camps. Here are two of the most popular areas people visit.

## The Côte d'Azur

For hot weather, go to the Côte d'Azur. (It is also known as the Riviera.) There are sandy beaches and you can swim in the warm Mediterranean sea.

There are three coast roads to choose from between Nice and Menton. The highest, known as the Great Corniche, winds through the mountains giving amazing views of the coast.

Villages were often built on hill-tops and fortified to be safe from attack. At St-Paul, there is a superb view of the sea from the old town walls.

St-Paul

Grasse

Biot

Nice

Monte Carlo

Menton

At the perfume factory in Grasse you can see how oil is taken from flowers to make perfume.

Vallauris

At the model park in Nice, there are models of ancient buildings and scenes showing how people used to live.

At the museum in Monte Carlo, there are very old clockwork dolls that still work.

At Biot you can visit the glassworks. They show you how glass is blown and cut.

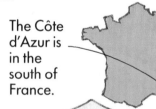

The Côte d'Azur is in the south of France.

Vallauris is famous for pottery. You can see pots being made in the traditional way, baked over a wood fire.

*Bouillabaisse* is a delicious soup made with many sorts of fish.

## Boating

Canals and rivers crisscross the whole of France. Boating holidays are a good way to see the countryside. You could hire a bicycle to go exploring nearby.

## Camping

Camping is very popular. Campsites are often in a forest or by the beach. In some places you can camp on a farm.

# Brittany

Along the rocky coast of Brittany there are sandy bays, fishing villages and islands to visit. At festivals, the Bretons (people of Brittany) wear colourful local costumes.

**Places to stay**
Some people stay in hotels or *gîtes* (country cottages). In *gîtes*, you buy food and cook for yourself.

On the Crozon peninsula you can walk along high cliff paths and see huge waves crashing against the rocks.

Where you see a cemetery, an ossuary (where bones are kept) and a carved stone cross grouped round a church, this is called a parish close. This one is at St-Thégonnec.

There are lighthouses along rocky parts of the coast. You can tour some of them.

There are boat trips from St-Malo. Cross the bay to Dinard, a seaside resort, or go up the river to the old town of Dinan.

*Galettes* are pancakes made with special flour called buckwheat. Eat them with a savoury filling or with jam.

In many places, such as Locranon, you can watch a religious procession, called a *pardon*. People wear traditional costume and carry candles, banners and statues of saints.

At Dinan there is a castle and a museum. You can see Breton costumes at the museum.

Breton women's costumes have lace head dresses. There are many styles such as this one, from Pont-l'Abbé.

In fields near Carnac, there are thousands of gigantic prehistoric standing stones, called menhirs.

From Vannes, boat trips tour the Morbihan Gulf. It is dotted with fishing boats and small islands.

Brittany is in the north-west of France.

At La Baule there is a five km long sandy beach.

St-Thégonnec

Crozon

Locronan

Pont-l'Abbé

Cap Fréhel

St-Malo

Dinan

Carnac

La Baule

# The story of France 1.

Long ago the first people in France lived in caves.

**40,000 BC**

They used charcoal, animal fats and crushed berries to make pictures on the walls of the animals they hunted.

**1000 BC**

The first settlers were tribes from the east. One tribe became known as the Gauls. The old name for France is Gaul, which comes from them.

This is Vercingétorix, the leader of the Gauls. The Roman army, led by Julius Caesar, defeated him and conquered Gaul.

**50 BC**

## Invaders

This map shows how France was invaded by tribes and armies from many directions. The Romans were the only invaders to spread throughout the land.

The Romans settled all over Gaul. They built towns of stone and brick. They farmed the land.

**AD 486**

The Romans were defeated by a tribe called the Franks. Their king, Clovis, called his new land France.

**AD 800**

Many years later, another king of the Franks called Charlemagne, conquered much of Europe. He was made Emperor. He set up the first schools.

**AD 845**

Norsemen came by sea in longboats and settled in northern France. They became known as Normans.

**AD 1066**

The Normans called their land Normandy. They built fortresses to keep out enemies. Their leader, Duke William, was very powerful.

## The Romans in Gaul

The Romans made buildings of stone all over Gaul. You can still see many of them.

You can still see plays at this theatre. It was built so cleverly that a whisper can be clearly heard.

## Roman roads

The Romans built many roads in Gaul. They were wide and straight.

Soldiers marched along the roads to reach all parts of Gaul quickly.

This is an aqueduct, a bridge carrying water pipes across a valley. You can walk along the top — if you have a head for heights.

Orange

Pont du Gard

There are pictures carved on this stone arch. They show Caesar's army fighting the Gauls.

This temple is the Maison Carrée. People came to pray here.

Nîmes

At Nîmes, look out for the chained crocodile symbol on buildings. It celebrates a Roman victory in Egypt.

Arles

Each July, this Roman theatre is used for a folk dancing festival.

Gladiator and animal fights were held in this arena.

This is an obelisk. Chariot races were run round it.

All these remains are in the south of France.

## The Bayeux tapestry

Harold is crowned king. Then a comet appears in the sky. People think it is a bad sign.

During the battle, William raises his helmet to show his men he is still alive.

An arrow pierces Harold's eye. He dies instantly.

In 1066, the Normans invaded Britain. Duke William defeated the English King Harold at the Battle of Hastings.

He became known as William the Conqueror. The Bayeux tapestry tells the story of the invasion.

The rest of the story of France is on the next page.

# The story of France 2

The next 500 years after the Normans came, are known as the Middle Ages. Dukes and kings ruled different parts of France. They fought each other. At last, one king ruled all of France.

**1226**

King Louis IX was such a good man, he became known as "Saint Louis". He would sit under an oak tree in the forest and poor people came to him for justice.

## The castles of the Loire valley

Near the River Loire, there are lots of *châteaux* (castles) to visit.

At first castles were built as fortresses, with a moat and drawbridge. Later, François I built fine palaces and hunting lodges, like those he had seen in Italy.

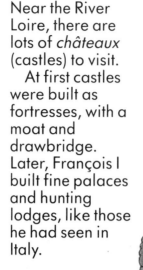

Ussé is like a fairytale castle in a forest. It is where Sleeping Beauty is supposed to have slept for a hundred years.

Chinon castle is made up of three fortresses. They are separated by moats. Joan of Arc came here to tell the king that God wanted her to lead the French army.

**1429**

France fought a 100 Years' War with England. A girl named Joan of Arc believed God meant her to save France. She led the French army to victory. Later, the French turned against her with the English. They said she was a witch and burnt her at the stake.

**1643**

King Louis XIV called himself the "Sun King". He thought he was like the sun, shining brightly on the people. He had a magnificent palace built near Paris, at Versailles.

**1789**

The poor people started a revolution, to get rid of the king. A mob attacked the Bastille prison, symbol of King Louis XVI's power. The king and queen were captured and guillotined.

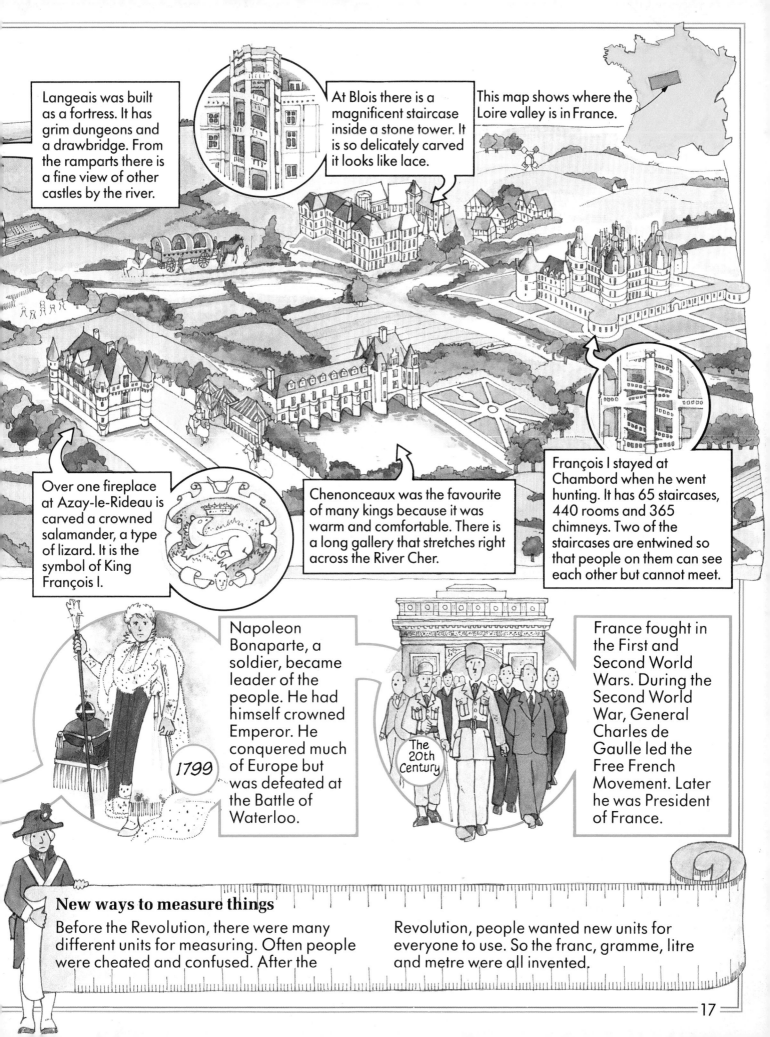

Langeais was built as a fortress. It has grim dungeons and a drawbridge. From the ramparts there is a fine view of other castles by the river.

At Blois there is a magnificent staircase inside a stone tower. It is so delicately carved it looks like lace.

This map shows where the Loire valley is in France.

Over one fireplace at Azay-le-Rideau is carved a crowned salamander, a type of lizard. It is the symbol of King François I.

Chenonceaux was the favourite of many kings because it was warm and comfortable. There is a long gallery that stretches right across the River Cher.

François I stayed at Chambord when he went hunting. It has 65 staircases, 440 rooms and 365 chimneys. Two of the staircases are entwined so that people on them can see each other but cannot meet.

Napoleon Bonaparte, a soldier, became leader of the people. He had himself crowned Emperor. He conquered much of Europe but was defeated at the Battle of Waterloo.

1799

The 20th Century

France fought in the First and Second World Wars. During the Second World War, General Charles de Gaulle led the Free French Movement. Later he was President of France.

## New ways to measure things

Before the Revolution, there were many different units for measuring. Often people were cheated and confused. After the Revolution, people wanted new units for everyone to use. So the franc, gramme, litre and metre were all invented.

# Paris

Paris is the capital city of France. It is an exciting place to visit. It has wide streets called *boulevards*, crowded narrow alleys and hundreds of cafés on the pavements. The River Seine flows through the city. Many old bridges cross the river. Along the banks there are lots of markets and bookstalls.

There are good views across the city from places marked like this on the map

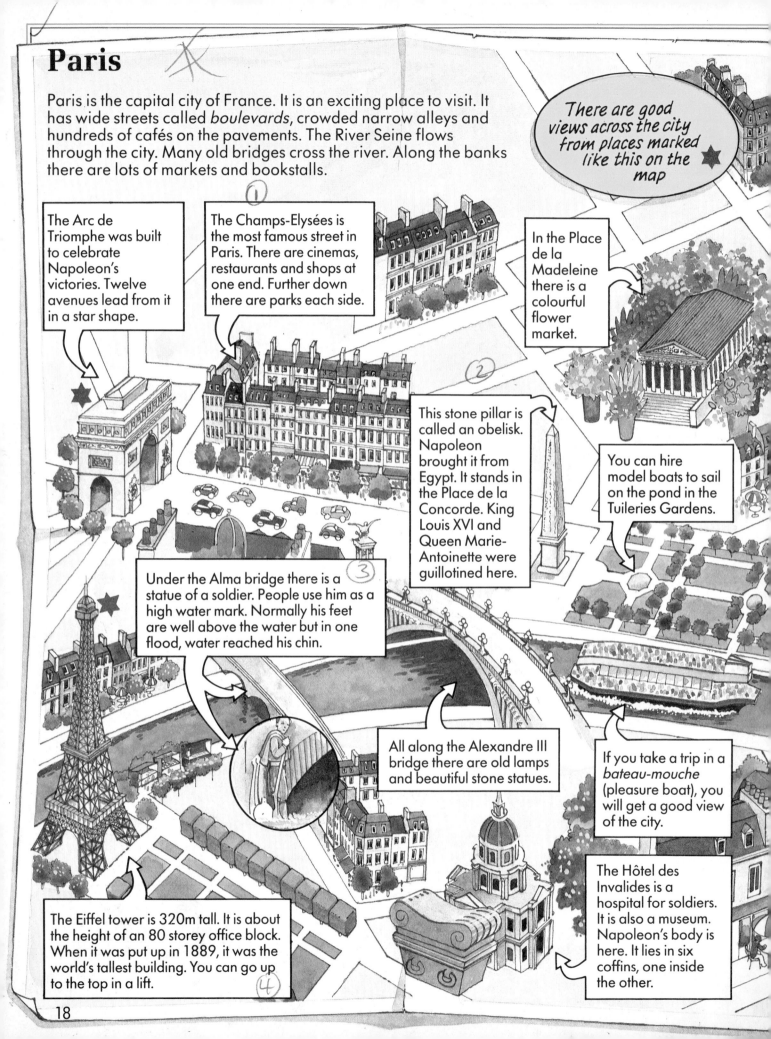

The Arc de Triomphe was built to celebrate Napoleon's victories. Twelve avenues lead from it in a star shape.

The Champs-Elysées is the most famous street in Paris. There are cinemas, restaurants and shops at one end. Further down there are parks each side.

In the Place de la Madeleine there is a colourful flower market.

This stone pillar is called an obelisk. Napoleon brought it from Egypt. It stands in the Place de la Concorde. King Louis XVI and Queen Marie-Antoinette were guillotined here.

You can hire model boats to sail on the pond in the Tuileries Gardens.

Under the Alma bridge there is a statue of a soldier. People use him as a high water mark. Normally his feet are well above the water but in one flood, water reached his chin.

All along the Alexandre III bridge there are old lamps and beautiful stone statues.

If you take a trip in a *bateau-mouche* (pleasure boat), you will get a good view of the city.

The Eiffel tower is 320m tall. It is about the height of an 80 storey office block. When it was put up in 1889, it was the world's tallest building. You can go up to the top in a lift.

The Hôtel des Invalides is a hospital for soldiers. It is also a museum. Napoleon's body is here. It lies in six coffins, one inside the other.

The Opéra is one of the largest theatres in the world. A vast chandelier inside weighs six tons, as much as an elephant.

Montmartre is an area of narrow, cobbled streets. Famous artists such as Picasso and Renoir used to paint here. Artists still crowd the area. In the Place du Tertre you can have your portrait drawn in a few minutes.

There are two ways to reach the Sacré-Coeur church. Take the funicular railway from the Place St-Pierre, or climb the steps.

This gigantic sphere is called the Géode. It is in the "Science City" on the outskirts of Paris. Inside is a cinema with a huge, curved screen. It makes you feel part of the film.

The Louvre was once a royal palace. Since the Revolution, it has been a museum. A huge glass pyramid stands in one courtyard.
    The Mona Lisa is a famous painting in the Louvre. People say she has a mysterious smile.

The Pompidou Centre is a museum and art gallery. Over the outside of the building run pipes for water, air and electricity, and escalators. Nearby, street artists perform and there are strange fountains to see.

Paris gets its name from a Celtic tribe, the Parisii. They settled here on an island. Later, the Romans built a city. They called it Lutetia, which means "City of Light" in Latin.

Distances from Paris to all towns in France are measured from Notre-Dame cathedral. It has huge flying buttresses, which are arches supporting the walls. Napoleon crowned himself here in 1804.

The *Pont Neuf* (New Bridge) is actually the oldest bridge in Paris. Long ago, acrobats and musicians performed here.

ILE DE LA CITE

ILE-ST-LOUIS

Posters are stuck on columns because it is forbidden to fix them to walls.

A *crotinette* is a motorbike with a cleaning machine fixed behind. It cleans up dog mess as it goes.

On the Ile-St-Louis is a famous ice cream shop called Berthillon.

# Customs and festivals

The French have traditional ways of celebrating special occasions. Many festivals and holidays are for religious events, such as Christmas and Easter. The Roman Catholic church is the main religion in France.

All over France there are festivals for local events, such as the harvest.

## Festivals through the year

◀ A special cake is eaten for the festival of the three wise men. The person who finds the bean hidden in the cake is king or queen for the day.

*6 January*

*Shrove Tuesday*

◀ People hold a coin while they toss pancakes. This brings them luck and money for a year.

▲ Menton is a town famous for its lemon trees. They hold a procession there of models made of lemons.

## Christenings

◀ Guests at christenings are given sugared almonds, called *dragées*.

## Birthdays

◀ One of a French child's names is often a saint's name. Children celebrate their birthday and their saint's day.

## Weddings

◀ Most couples have two wedding ceremonies. They are married by the mayor in the town hall. They may have a church wedding too.

## Funerals

People put chrysanthemum flowers on the graves of relatives and friends.

◀ People give each other bunches of lily-of-the-valley for good luck.

*1 May*

*25 May*

At Saintes-Maries-de-la-Mer there ▶ is a gypsy festival. A statue of Saint Sarah is carried into the sea.

## Local costume

In many areas people dress in traditional costume for events such as folk-dancing.

Many costumes have colourful patterns and elaborate head dresses.

◀ Burgundy

◀ Savoy Alps

Provence

Massif ▶ Central

Alsace ▶

People celebrate the attack on the Bastille prison during the Revolution. They hold street parties and firework displays.

*14 July*

ST. MARY'S COLLEGE
BELFAST, 12.

# The Basque country

The Basque people live in the Pyrenees mountain region that joins France and Spain. They have their own language and traditions such as dances, songs and games. You can find out about the Basque way of life at the Basque Museum in Bayonne.

Bayonne •

Larressoe

Espelette

Mauléon

Gotein

• Tardets

At Bayonne, there is a carnival in July. They have bullfights and folk dancing.

Basque dances are lively and colourful. They are done mostly by men wearing local costume. The dancers often make great leaps into the air.

The game of pelota is played all over the Basque country. Players hold a wicker glove to hurl a ball against a high wall.

At Espelette, wild mountain ponies called *pottoks* are sold at a fair in January.

At Larressoe, they make swordsticks to be used in Basque dances.

Basque church towers often have three crosses at the top. This church is at Gotein.

At Mauléon, they make rope-soled canvas shoes, called *espadrilles*.

The Basques have their own flag.

The Basque region covers parts of France and Spain.

Basque men traditionally wear a black beret. They wear a red beret for Basque dances.

You can see the hobby-horse dance at a festival in August at Tardets.

September — In the wine regions they end the grape harvest with dances and wine-tasting.

24 December — ◀ Many families go to church for midnight mass. In the south of France, people bring live lambs and lay them by the crib.

The traditional Christmas cake is a chocolate "log", filled with cream. ▼

25 December

At midnight, ▶ car drivers blow their horns to wish each other a Happy New Year.

31 December

# Shops and markets

French people like to eat food that is very fresh. They buy food every day in local shops. Many people go to a supermarket once a week. Most shops close for two hours at lunchtime, especially in the south where it is hot.

## At the baker's shop

A shop that sells bread and cakes is called a *boulangerie-pâtisserie.* French people buy bread once or even twice a day, as it does not stay fresh for long. Most bread is white. Many loaves are baked in shapes that have names to match, as shown below.

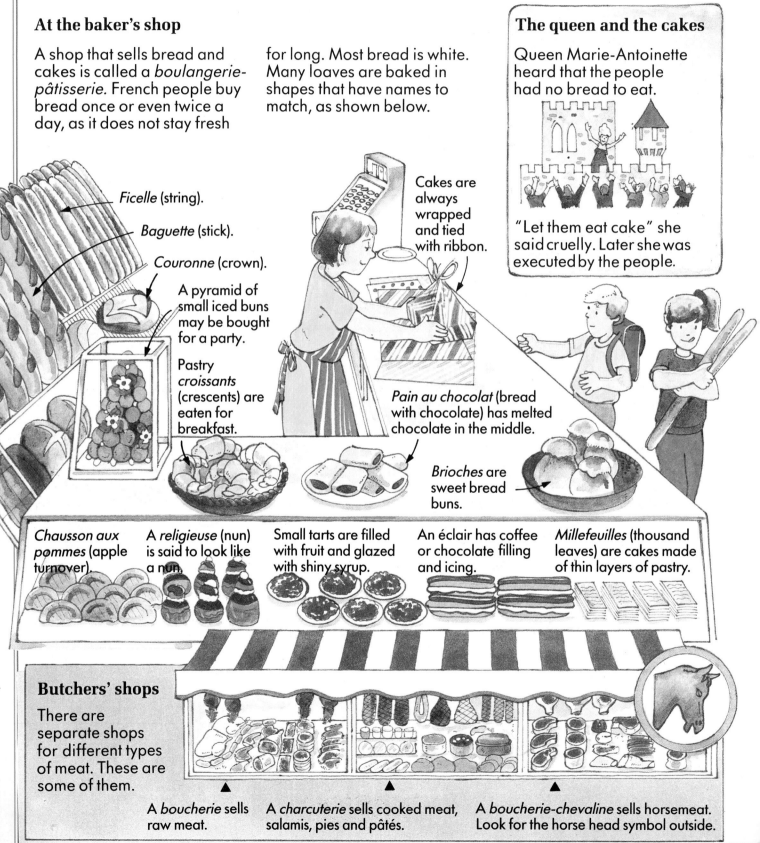

*Ficelle* (string).

*Baguette* (stick).

*Couronne* (crown).

A pyramid of small iced buns may be bought for a party.

Pastry *croissants* (crescents) are eaten for breakfast.

Cakes are always wrapped and tied with ribbon.

*Pain au chocolat* (bread with chocolate) has melted chocolate in the middle.

*Brioches* are sweet bread buns.

### The queen and the cakes

Queen Marie-Antoinette heard that the people had no bread to eat.

"Let them eat cake" she said cruelly. Later she was executed by the people.

*Chausson aux pommes* (apple turnover).

A *religieuse* (nun) is said to look like a nun.

Small tarts are filled with fruit and glazed with shiny syrup.

An éclair has coffee or chocolate filling and icing.

*Millefeuilles* (thousand leaves) are cakes made of thin layers of pastry.

## Butchers' shops

There are separate shops for different types of meat. These are some of them.

A *boucherie* sells raw meat.

A *charcuterie* sells cooked meat, salamis, pies and pâtés.

A *boucherie-chevaline* sells horsemeat. Look for the horse head symbol outside.

## Market day

Most towns have weekly markets. All sorts of other things are for sale besides food. Many food stalls let you taste before you buy.

Part of the market may be in a covered hall.

Stalls are set up throughout the town.

Traders call out to passers-by to stop and buy.

Many stalls have just one sort of food. This man is selling oysters from buckets of ice.

Fruit is often displayed with its leaves to show how fresh it is.

This farmer sells cheese made with milk from her own goat.

Olives may be spiced or flavoured with herbs.

### French money

Money in France consists of francs and centimes. 100 centimes make one franc.

French bank notes have pictures of famous Frenchmen on them. On the 20 franc note is Claude Debussy, a composer.

Some French coins.

Live rabbits and chickens are for sale here.

People buy strings of onions to hang in the kitchen, ready to use.

This man is showing people a new kitchen gadget.

23

# Sports and outdoor activities

There are many outdoor things to do in France.

- Sports and famous events you can watch are shown like this on the map.

- This symbol means you can take part yourself.

Horse racing and soccer are the only sports in France at which people can bet. There is a famous racecourse at Longchamp.

The Tour de France is a cycle race. It goes all over France and follows a new route each year. Crowds line the roads and applaud the winners at the end in Paris.

Cycling is a great way to see the countryside. You can hire bicycles at most railway stations.

Paris

Huge waves can make swimming dangerous on the Atlantic coast. Many beaches have coloured flags to tell you when it is safe to swim.

At Le Mans there is a 24 hour car race. Each car has two or three drivers who take turns.

Soccer is the most popular sport. St Etienne is one of the best teams.

The Ardèche river flows very fast in places. People enjoy canoeing down it.

Many people go skiing in winter. One of the world's longest ski runs is in the French Alps.

Rugby is especially popular in southern France, where most towns and villages have a team.

Cross-country skiing is popular in areas of the mountains where the slopes are not too steep.

Bullfights are held in the Roman arenas at Nîmes and Arles.

## The game of *boules*

*Boules* is a traditional game which can be played on any flat patch of ground. Each player throws two metal balls towards a smaller ball called a *cochonnet* (piglet).

The ball closest to the *cochonnet* is the winner.

## Outdoor places to visit

Here are some places to explore out-of-doors. Some of them have special children's activities.

### Gardens

Many castles have beautiful gardens. They are often laid out in patterns.

The garden at Villandry castle has three terraces. It looks like gardens of King Louis XIV's time, 300 years ago.

Monet, a famous French artist, painted this water lily pond many times. It is in his garden at Giverny.

### Amusement parks

Some amusement parks are based on themes such as science, fantasy and well-known cartoon characters.

You can take part in the adventures of the cartoon character Asterix the Gaul, at the Asterix Park near Paris. There is a model of his village in Gaul where you can meet him and his friend Obelix.

### Scenic railways and cable cars

Miniature railways and cable cars can take you high up into the mountains. Cable cars are used a lot by skiers and hikers.

The funicular (cable) railway from St Hilaire-du-Touvet is the steepest climbing railway in Europe.

Giverny · Asterix Park
Paris
Villandry
Chamonix
Lascaux St-Hilaire
Padirac
Aven Armand
Camargue

### Caves

Most of the underground caves to visit are in southern France.

At Lascaux II, you can see copies of the finest prehistoric cave paintings in France.

The world's tallest stalagmite is in the Aven Armand cave.
Take a boat along an underground river at Padirac.

You can take an exciting ride by cable car from Chamonix for a good view of Mont Blanc.

Each January, racing drivers set off from all over Europe for the Monte Carlo Rally.

### National parks

Many areas of forest, mountains, rivers and lakes are national parks. They are good places for seeing nature.

The Camargue is a marshy area where wild white horses and black bulls live. Men on horseback control the bulls which are kept for bullfights.

# Famous French people

There have been many famous French people in the past. You can find out about some of them, such as Napoleon, on other pages. Most of the famous people described here lived in the last 100 years. Two of them are not real people. Can you tell which two?

Claude Debussy was a composer and pianist. He wrote a well-known tune for piano called *Au Clair de la Lune.*

◄ Auguste Rodin was a sculptor. You can see many of his sculptures at the Rodin Museum in Paris. This one is called The Thinker.

## Impressionist painters

The Impressionists were a group of artists. They painted their impressions instead of trying to paint exactly what they saw. Many of them painted scenes near Paris and in the south of France.

◄ Charles Blondin was a tight-rope walker. In 1859 he crossed the Niagara Falls, a gigantic waterfall in North America.

◄ Charlotte Corday was a famous murderess. She stabbed Marat, a leader of the Revolution, in his bath. She was caught and beheaded at the guillotine.

Auguste Renoir was an Impressionist painter. Many of his pictures show people having fun. He painted people at the theatre and dancing, for instance.

Marcel Marceau is a brilliant mime artist. He often plays Pierrot, a French pantomime character.

◄ Coco Chanel designed elegant women's clothes. A perfume called Chanel No. 5 was created for her.

Edgar Degas is well-known for his pictures of race horses and ballet dancers.
  Many Impressionist paintings are in the Orsay Museum in Paris.

◄ On some French stamps and coins there is a picture of an imaginary woman called Marianne. She is the symbol of the French Republic and her statue is in every town hall in France.

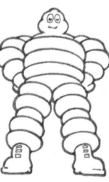

The Michelin Man is the symbol of a French tyre company, called Michelin. You can see him on cars and trucks and on Michelin guide books and maps.

## Writers

La Fontaine wrote popular fables. *The Grasshopper and the Ant* is a story of a hard-working ant and a lazy grasshopper.

Victor Hugo wrote many stories. *Notre-Dame-de-Paris* is about Quasimodo, a hunchback. He lived in the belfry of Notre-Dame cathedral.

## Film stars

Brigitte Bardot was a popular film star during the 1960s. Nowadays she is well-known for her animal rights campaigns.

Jacques Tati was a film director and actor. He made comedy films including *Monsieur Hulot's Holiday*, about an accident-prone man in a hotel.

## Inventors

Louis Braille was blind from when he was three. He invented a system of raised dots on a page for blind people to "read" with their fingers. It is called Braille.

Louis Pasteur was a chemist. He discovered that germs cause disease. He also invented the process of "pasteurization", used for killing germs in milk.

Marie Curie was a scientist. Together with her husband Pierre, she discovered the substances polonium and radium. Radium is sometimes used in treating cancer.

Louis and Auguste Lumière invented a machine for showing moving films. They made the first film shown in a cinema.

Jacques Cousteau invented the aqualung, used by divers for breathing underwater. He has made many films about his underwater adventures.

## Sportsmen

Michel Platini is France's best-known footballer. He played for Bordeaux and was European Footballer of the Year three times.

Jean-Claude Killy is a skier. He won all four World Cup titles in 1967 and three gold medals in the 1968 Winter Olympics.

# More things to do in France

Here are some more places to visit in France. All the ones on this page are near Paris.

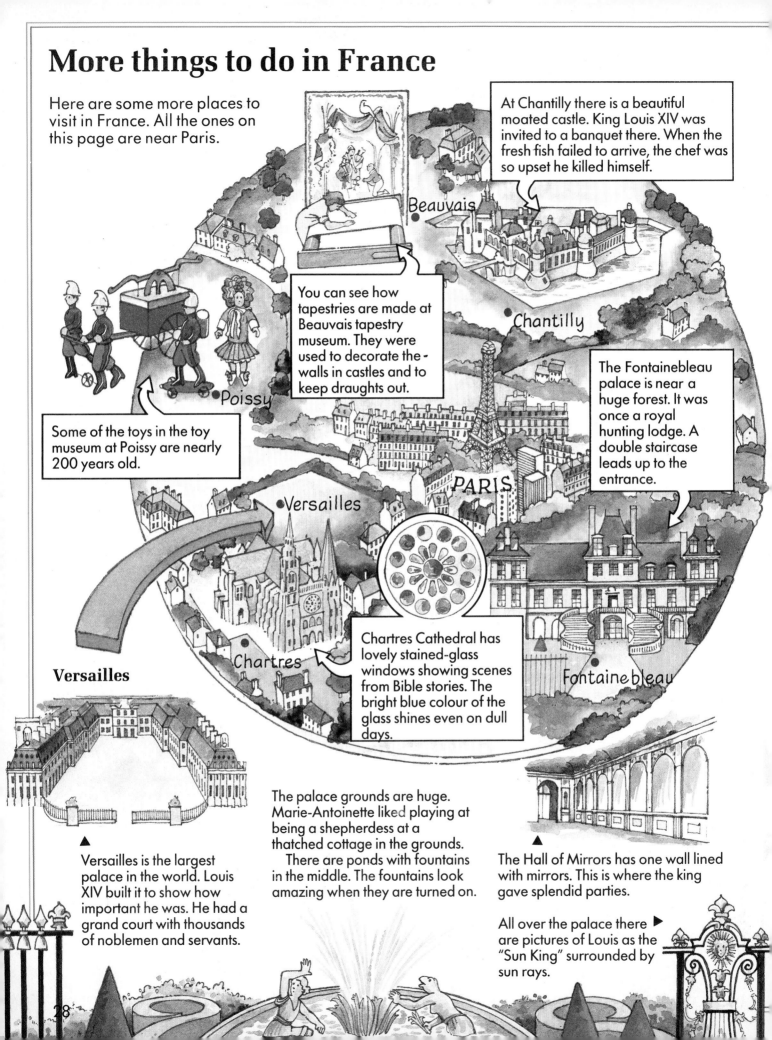

At Chantilly there is a beautiful moated castle. King Louis XIV was invited to a banquet there. When the fresh fish failed to arrive, the chef was so upset he killed himself.

You can see how tapestries are made at Beauvais tapestry museum. They were used to decorate the walls in castles and to keep draughts out.

The Fontainebleau palace is near a huge forest. It was once a royal hunting lodge. A double staircase leads up to the entrance.

Some of the toys in the toy museum at Poissy are nearly 200 years old.

Chartres Cathedral has lovely stained-glass windows showing scenes from Bible stories. The bright blue colour of the glass shines even on dull days.

## Versailles

Versailles is the largest palace in the world. Louis XIV built it to show how important he was. He had a grand court with thousands of noblemen and servants.

The palace grounds are huge. Marie-Antoinette liked playing at being a shepherdess at a thatched cottage in the grounds.

There are ponds with fountains in the middle. The fountains look amazing when they are turned on.

The Hall of Mirrors has one wall lined with mirrors. This is where the king gave splendid parties.

All over the palace there ▶ are pictures of Louis as the "Sun King" surrounded by sun rays.

## Other interesting places

### Arromanches

At Arromanches there are the remains of a harbour. It was built for landing British troops during the Second World War. There is a model of the harbour in the Invasion Museum.

### Blois

At Blois you can visit a chocolate factory. A popular brand called Poulain is made there.

### Lyon

In the puppet museum at Lyon, there are lots of puppets of a famous comic character, named Guignol. He is a drunken layabout from Lyon.

### Provence

In Provence, you may see craftsmen making small clay figures, called *santons.* Each one is dressed as a Nativity figure, or as a country character such as a milkmaid.

Arromanches

Blois

Lyon

Avignon

Provence

### Avignon

*Sur le Pont d'Avignon* (On the Bridge at Avignon) is a song about people dancing on a bridge. You can see the remains of this old bridge at Avignon.

The old part of Avignon is interesting. It was built in the Middle Ages. Some popes lived in the palace here, instead of in Rome.

### Sound and Light shows

On summer evenings there are *Son et Lumière* (Sound and Light) shows at many castles. They tell the story of the place with acting, music and lights.

### Wine cellars

In wine regions, you can often visit the cellars where the wine is made. Some cellars in the Champagne area are so big, you go round by electric train.

### Holiday scrapbook

Try keeping a scrapbook of France. Put in it stamps, food and drink labels, tickets, postcards and so on, and a map showing places you visited.

# Facts about France

France is a republic. This means it has an elected leader called the President. France first became a republic in 1792 after the Revolution in 1789, when the king was overthrown as leader. 14 July 1989 is the 200th anniversary of the Revolution.

Every seven years French people vote for a new President. A picture of the President hangs in every town hall.

WORLD RECORDS

◄ The French Parliament is made up of the National Assembly and the Senate. The National Assembly meets in The Chamber of Deputies (shown in the picture).

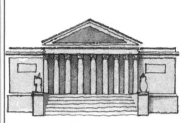

The *Tricolore* (Three-coloured) flag became the French flag at the time of the Revolution. It is red, white and blue. ▶

The longest rail tunnel in the world will be the Eurotunnel, due to open in 1993. It is being built under the English Channel to link Calais and Dover.

The National Anthem is called *The Marseillaise*. It was originally sung during the Revolution by soldiers from Marseille.

The largest nuclear reactor in the world is being built in France. The French have more nuclear power stations than any other country in Europe.

## Products

France has more farmland than any other country in Europe. Its largest crops are wheat, barley, grapes and apples.

In parts of France, especially in the north-east, there are huge factories. The main exports include machinery, aircraft and cars.

## Language

The French language is based on Latin, the language spoken by the Romans in Gaul. In some places people have local languages too. People in Brittany speak Breton and the Basque language is spoken in the Pyrenees, for example.

The world's only tidal power station is on the Rance estuary in Brittany. As the tide goes out, it turns machines that produce electricity.

# Regions

France is divided into 22 regions, including the island of Corsica. Each region has a name. Some of them date from the Middle Ages.

Some regions also have an English name. These are shown in brackets.

## Departments

France is also divided into 96 *départements* (departments). Most are named after the main river running through them and each one has a main town.

- 92
- 93
- 94
- 75

| | | |
|---|---|---|
| 01 Ain | 32 Gers | 66 Pyrénées- |
| 02 Aisne | 33 Gironde | Orientales |
| 03 Allier | 34 Hérault | 67 Bas-Rhin |
| 04 Alpes de | 35 Ille-et-Vilaine | 68 Haut-Rhin |
| Haute- | 36 Indre | 69 Rhône |
| Provence | 37 Indre-et-Loire | 70 Haute-Saône |
| 05 Hautes-Alpes | 38 Isère | 71 Saône-et-Loire |
| 06 Alpes- | 39 Jura | 72 Sarthe |
| Maritimes | 40 Landes | 73 Savoie |
| 07 Ardèche | 41 Loir-et-Cher | 74 Haute-Savoie |
| 08 Ardennes | 42 Loire | 75 Ville de Paris |
| 09 Ariège | 43 Haute-Loire | 76 Seine-Maritime |
| 10 Aube | 44 Loire- | 77 Seine-et-Marne |
| 11 Aude | Atlantique | 78 Yvelines |
| 12 Aveyron | 45 Loiret | 79 Deux-Sèvres |
| 13 Bouches-du- | 46 Lot | 80 Somme |
| Rhône | 47 Lot-et-Garonne | 81 Tarn |
| 14 Calvados | 48 Lozère | 82 Tarn-et- |
| 15 Cantal | 49 Maine-et-Loire | Garonne |
| 16 Charente | 50 Manche | 83 Var |
| 17 Charente- | 51 Marne | 84 Vaucluse |
| Maritime | 52 Haute-Marne | 85 Vendée |
| 18 Cher | 53 Mayenne | 86 Vienne |
| 19 Corrèze | 54 Meurthe-et- | 87 Haute-Vienne |
| 20 a Haute-Corse | Moselle | 88 Vosges |
| 20 b Corse-du-Sud | 55 Meuse | 89 Yonne |
| 21 Côte-d'Or | 56 Morbihan | 90 Territoire de |
| 22 Côtes-du-Nord | 57 Moselle | Belfort |
| 23 Creuse | 58 Nièvre | 91 Essonne |
| 24 Dordogne | 59 Nord | 92 Hauts-de-Seine |
| 25 Doubs | 60 Oise | 93 Seine-Saint- |
| 26 Drôme | 61 Orne | Denis |
| 27 Eure | 62 Pas-de-Calais | 94 Val-de-Marne |
| 28 Eure-et-Loire | 63 Puy-de-Dôme | 95 Val-d'Oise |
| 29 Finistère | 64 Pyrénées- | 96 Territoire |
| 30 Gard | Atlantique | d'Outre Mer |
| 31 Haute- | 65 Hautes- | |
| Garonne | Pyrénées | |

## Number-plate game

The last two numbers on French cars tell you which department the car is from.

Here is a game you can play on holiday in France. Write the department numbers down. Tick them off as you spot cars from each area. The winner is the person who has ticked the most departments by the end of the holiday.

## Quiz

Find the first letter of each department whose number is shown below. Can you rearrange the letters to spell the name of a popular holiday region in France?

69 13 59 89 01 81 82 36

# Index

First published in 1989 by Usborne Publishing Ltd, 20 Garrick Street, London WC2E 9BJ, England.

Copyright © Usborne Publishing Ltd, 1989.
The name Usborne and the device ♁ are Trade Marks of Usborne Publishing Ltd.

Asterix picture © 1989 Les Editions Albert René/Goscinny-Uderzo

All rights reserved. No part of this publication may be reproduced, stored in a retrieval system or transmitted in any form or by any means, electronic, mechanical, photocopying, recording or otherwise, without the prior permission of the publisher.

Printed in Belgium.